10 CLUMSY EMUS

Ken and Pam, always an inspiration—WB

Don't miss these other great books!

Scholastic Australia

345 Pacific Highway Lindfield NSW 2070

An imprint of Scholastic Australia Pty Limited

PO Box 579 Gosford NSW 2250

ABN 11 000 614 577

www.scholastic.com.au

Part of the Scholastic Group

Sydney • Auckland • New York • Toronto • London • Mexico City • New Delhi • Hong Kong • Buenos Aires • Puerto Rico

Published by Scholastic Australia in 2014.

Text copyright © Scholastic Australia, 2014.

Illustrations copyright © Wendy Binks, 2014.

National Library of Australia Cataloguing-in-Publication entry:

Author: Allen, Ed, author.

Title: 10 clumsy emus / Ed Allen; illustrated by Wendy Binks.

ISBN: 9781742836393 (paperback)

Target Audience: For pre-school age.

Subjects: Emus--Juvenile fiction.

     Counting.

     Picture books for children.

Other Authors/Contributors: Binks, Wendy, illustrator.

Dewey Number: A823.4

Typeset in Hunniwell, featuring Terylene.

Printed in China by RR Donnelley.

Scholastic Australia's policy, in association with RR Donnelley, is to use papers that are renewable and made efficiently from wood grown in sustainable forests, so as to minimise its environmental footprint.

10 9 8 7 6 5 4 3 2 1   14 15 16 17 18 / 1

10 CLUMSY EMUS

Ed Allen • Wendy Binks

A SCHOLASTIC AUSTRALIA BOOK

Ten clumsy emus rolling down the hill.

Ten clumsy emus rolling down the hill.

And if one clumsy emu should feel a little ill,

There'll be nine clumsy emus rolling down the hill.

Nine clumsy emus in a game of basketball.

Nine clumsy emus in a game of basketball.

And if one clumsy emu is just not very tall,

There'll be eight clumsy emus in a game of basketball.

Eight clumsy emus playing musical chairs.
Eight clumsy emus playing musical chairs.
And if one clumsy emu needs to make repairs,
There'll be seven clumsy emus playing musical chairs.

Seven clumsy emus flying model planes.

Seven clumsy emus flying model planes.

And if one clumsy emu breaks the window panes,
There'll be six clumsy emus flying model planes.

Six clumsy emus making paper shapes.
Six clumsy emus making paper shapes.

And if one clumsy emu gets tangled in the tape,
There'll be five clumsy emus making paper shapes.

Five clumsy emus paddling on the lake.
Five clumsy emus paddling on the lake.
And if one clumsy emu makes a big mistake,
There'll be four clumsy emus paddling on the lake.

Four clumsy emus tidying their room.
Four clumsy emus tidying their room.

And if one clumsy emu should sneak away too soon,
There'll be three clumsy emus tidying their room.

Three clumsy emus visiting the zoo.
Three clumsy emus visiting the zoo.

And if one clumsy emu accidentally stays there too,
There'll be two clumsy emus visiting the zoo.

TWO clumsy emus making big mud pies.
Two clumsy emus making big mud pies.

And if one clumsy emu should swat at pesky flies,
There'll be one clumsy emu making big mud pies.

one clumsy emu having a bubble bath.

One clumsy emu having a bubble bath.

And if that clumsy emu floats right down the path,
There'll be no clumsy emus having a bubble bath.

Ten clumsy emus having a sing-a-long.

Ten clumsy emus having a sing-a-long.

And if all those clumsy emus sing this very song,

There'll be ten clumsy emus having a sing-a-long!